For Lincoln Students!.
1996

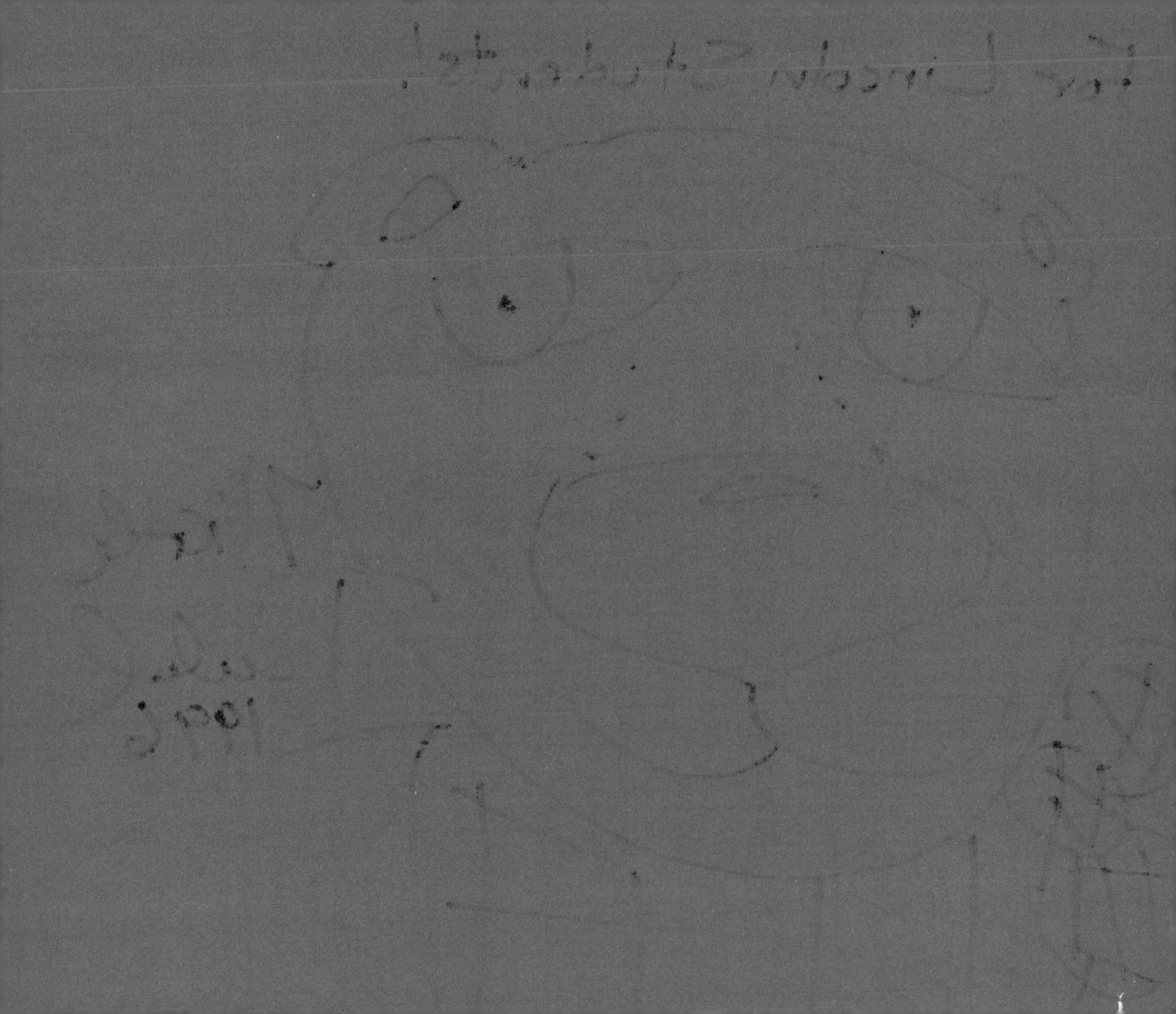

CYRANO THE BEAR

story and pictures by Nicole Rubel

Dial Books for Young Readers  New York

Published by Dial Books for Young Readers
A Division of Penguin Books USA Inc.
375 Hudson Street | New York, New York 10014

Designed by Amelia Lau Carling
Printed in Hong Kong
First Edition
1 3 5 7 9 10 8 6 4 2

Library of Congress Cataloging in Publication Data
Rubel, Nicole. Cyrano the bear /
story and pictures by Nicole Rubel.—1st ed. p. cm.
Summary: Although he is the bravest sheriff in the West,
Cyrano is afraid to let Roxane, the town librarian,
know that he has been writing love poems to her while
trying to capture the Gila Monster Gang.
ISBN 0-8037-1444-0.—ISBN 0-8037-1445-9 (lib. bdg.)
[1. West (U.S.)—Fiction. 2. Animals—Fiction.
3. Self-confidence—Fiction.]
I. Title. PZ7.R828Cy 1995 [E]—dc20 94-25902 CIP AC

The artwork for this book was created with black ink and watercolor paints.
It was then color-separated and reproduced in full color.

For all young buckaroos and buckarettes

Cyrano was the bravest sheriff in the West. He could lasso a varmint at forty paces, but he got all tangled up when he thought about Roxane, the town librarian.

Unfortunately Cyrano had been born with an enormous nose.

When he was young, some of the kids made fun of him. He tried to hide his huge nose under a large cowboy hat.

In school, however, his teacher, Miss Gopher, found that Cyrano had a special talent. "Cyrano, you write such beautiful poetry," she said.

Now that he was grown up, Cyrano wrote poems to Roxane every Valentine's Day. He signed them, "Your Secret Admirer." Although Roxane didn't know who had sent them, she loved the valentines and slept with them tucked inside her pillow.

But Roxane, with her cloud of curls, pink ears, and dainty hooves, was admired by everyone. Especially by Wolfie, Sheriff Cyrano's handsome deputy.

One day handsome Deputy Wolfie was overseeing the kissing booth at the county fair, while Sheriff Cyrano was helping out at the ringtoss. Suddenly the town bell clanged, warning the lawmen that there was trouble.

The Gila Monster Gang had burst into town.

Terrorizing everyone, they robbed the bank, the general store, and the post office.

The bandits galloped away, leaving behind a cloud of dust. Sneezing and coughing, Sheriff Cyrano had to stop. His great nose had filled with dust. He and Deputy Wolfie returned to the jailhouse empty-handed.

While Sheriff Cyrano blew his nose, Deputy Wolfie sighed. "Could you help me write a valentine for Roxane?" he asked. "I can't think of a thing to say."

At first Cyrano wanted to refuse. But Wolfie seemed so unhappy that the kindhearted Cyrano, who had already written his own secret valentine to Roxane, wrote another flowery poem. Wolfie signed his name to it.

The next day Roxane got two valentines that sounded very much alike! Earlier one had sailed through her window, and now Deputy Wolfie handed her another one.

"Holy tumbleweeds!" she exclaimed. "Both of these valentines are in the same handwriting. I'll bet Deputy Wolfie is my secret admirer!" Excitedly she sent Wolfie a note asking him to send her one more poem.

Roxane's note arrived just as Cyrano and Wolfie returned from yet another unsuccessful chase after the Gila Monster Gang. As Cyrano grabbed a handkerchief and sneezed, Wolfie read Roxane's note. "She wants another poem!" he cried.

"Forget it! We have to worry about bandits now!" snapped Cyrano as he went over to the saloon to get a sarsaparilla for his dry throat.

"Please!" begged Wolfie, following him. "You know I can't write poetry." He was desperate. Cyrano sighed, thinking bitterly that Roxane would always prefer the handsome deputy anyway, so he wrote another poem for him. Wolfie took it and went to slip it under Roxane's door.

Cyrano felt heartsick after writing the second poem for Wolfie. To take his mind off his troubles, he decided to redouble his efforts to catch the Gila Monster Gang. He thought he would ride over to see Buffalo Wise Woman and ask her advice.

After hearing about the slippery Gila Monster Gang, Buffalo Wise Woman said, "I see steam and railroad tracks."

"The train from Santa Fe!" said Cyrano. "But where?"

"I see violet-colored boulders and rushing water," she replied.

"Whoa now!" said Cyrano. "The Gila Monster Gang's going to rob the train at Purple Rock River!"

"By the way, I give all sorts of advice," said Buffalo Wise Woman. "I sense a longing in your heart for the beautiful Roxane. Don't hide behind your nose, Cyrano. Faint heart ne'er won fair lady. A big nose is a small excuse for being afraid to speak up. Tell Roxane your true feelings."

Cyrano thanked Buffalo Wise Woman for her advice. With his sharp sense of smell he sniffed the air for train smoke, and galloped off toward Purple Rock River.

When he got to the river, he saw the Gang already robbing the train!

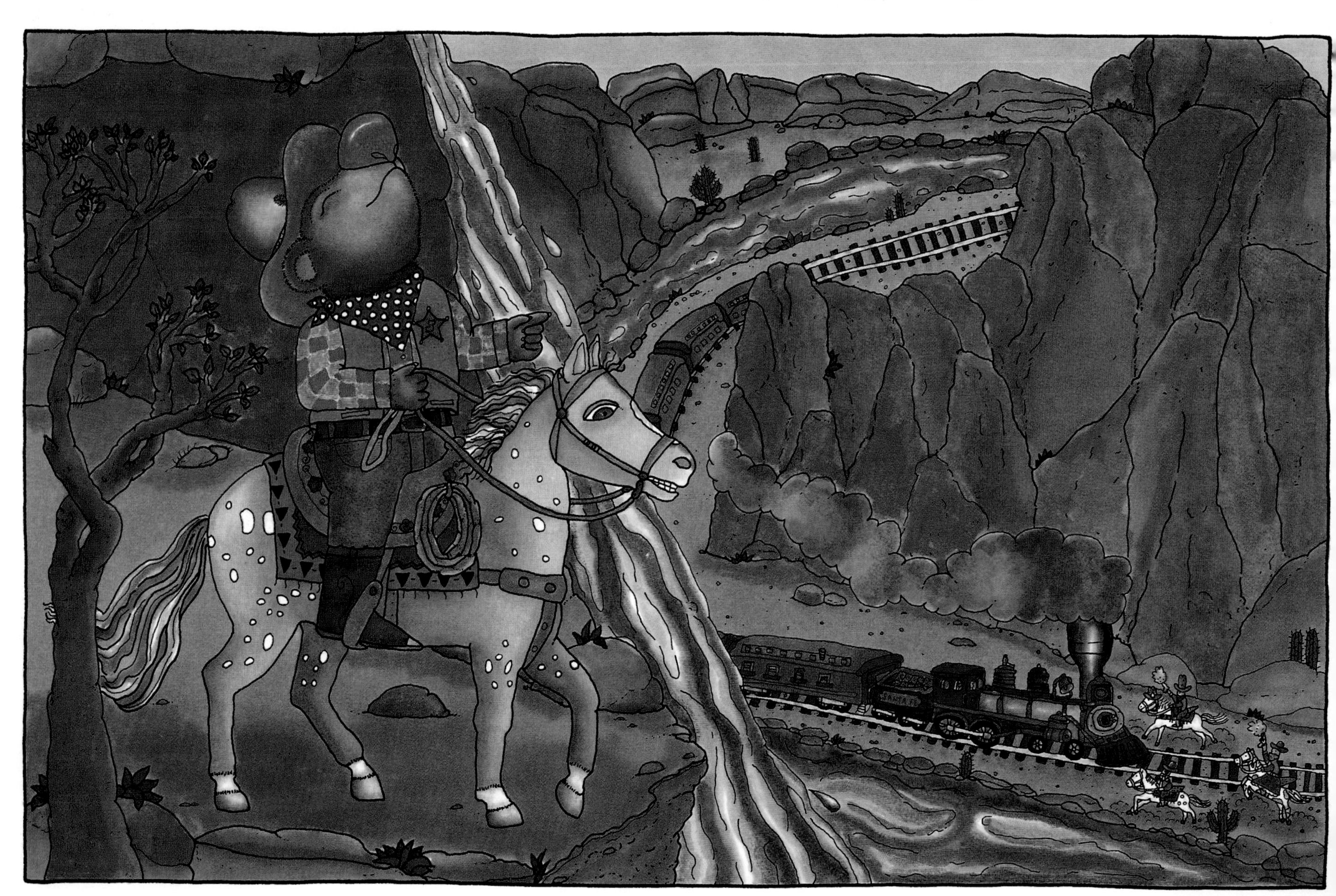

Cyrano dove into the water and snorkled along until he was directly behind the Gang's leader.

Leaping out of the water, Cyrano poked the robber sharply in the back with his nose and growled, "Stick 'em up!"

The rest of the Gang ran to help their leader. Pulling out his lasso, Cyrano roped them all together with one magnificent throw!

In the meantime Roxane had asked Deputy Wolfie to come to her house.
"Say something sweet and poetic to me," she commanded coyly.
"Howdy," said Wolfie.
"Is that all you can say?" she asked.
"Howdy, ma'am?" he said hopefully.

"Tell me about writing your valentines," she sighed.

"I can't remember," said Wolfie, shifting nervously on the sofa. Suddenly the town bell rang, and Wolfie jumped up. "Got to go," he said, glad for an excuse to escape. "I'm on duty."

"I'm coming too," said Roxane, determined not to give up so easily.

Wolfie and Roxane arrived just in time to see Cyrano leading the Gila Monster Gang to jail. He was making them march to a poem he'd just made up:

"As the sheriff with the biggest snout,
don't you doubt, I've got the clout
to fill the jail with you three louts!"

Something about the poem clicked in Roxane's head. "That rhythm! That meter! Cyrano is a poet!" Then it dawned on her. "Cyrano is *the* poet! *Cyrano* is my secret admirer!"

"It's true," said Buffalo Wise Woman, who had also come to see Cyrano's triumphant capture of the Gila Monster Gang. "Cyrano fears you will never love him because of his enormous nose!"

"Cyrano! Your great nose has taught you to be courageous, but your poetry has lassoed my heart!" exclaimed Roxane.

Roxane and Cyrano were married on Valentine's Day. And ever after, over campfires, ballads are sung about the brave Cyrano with his enormous nose and his beautiful bride, Roxane.